HUNTER ON HOLIDAY

A BIG TRIP AROUND EUROPE

JESSICA AND STEPHEN
PARRY-VALENTINE

PUFFIN BOOKS

ILLUSTRATED BY
ASHLEE SPINK

PUFFIN BOOKS

UK | USA | Canada | Ireland | Australia
India | New Zealand | South Africa | China

Penguin Random House Australia is part of the Penguin Random House group of companies whose addresses can be found at global.penguinrandomhouse.com.

First published by Puffin Books, an imprint of Penguin Random House Australia Pty Ltd, in 2023

Cover and internal design by Rebecca King © Penguin Random House Australia Pty Ltd

Printed and bound in China

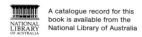 A catalogue record for this book is available from the National Library of Australia

ISBN 978 1 76 104692 6 (Hardback)

Penguin Random House Australia uses papers that are natural and recyclable products, made from wood grown in sustainable forests. The logging and manufacture processes are expected to conform to the environmental regulations of the country of origin.

penguin.com.au

We at Penguin Random House Australia acknowledge that Aboriginal and Torres Strait Islander peoples are the Traditional Custodians and the first storytellers of the lands on which we live and work. We honour Aboriginal and Torres Strait Islander peoples' continuous connection to Country, waters, skies and communities. We celebrate Aboriginal and Torres Strait Islander stories, traditions and living cultures; and we pay our respects to Elders past and present.

I have a long, long list of places that I want see.
There are just so many adventures out there waiting for me.

Our bags are all packed, we have passports in tow.
We're checked in and waiting. It's almost time to go!

TIME	DESTINATIONS	GATE	REMARKS
06:00	LONDON	30	BOARDING
06:45	PARIS	5	BOARDING
07:00	BARCELONA	23	BOARDING
07:25	HELSINKI	8	GO TO GATE
08:00	TOKYO	9	BOARDING
08:30	COPENHAGEN	21	GO TO GATE
08:45	EDINBURGH	32	ON TIME
09:00	ROME	7	ON TIME
09:15	ATHENS	15	CANCELLED
09:45	ISTANBUL	18	DELAYED
10:00	TORONTO	25	ON TIME
10:15	SEOUL	7	DELAYED
10:30	NEW YOR	2	DELAYED
10:45	BERLIN		ANCELLED
11:15	SYDNEY		NCELLED
11:30	REYKJAVIK		N TIME

Our luggage is stowed, and we buckle seatbelts quick smart.
The plane is taking off now, our trip is about to start!

I want to go to England where the hills roll in shades of green,
Munch on cucumber sandwiches and scones with clotted cream.

I want to go to Scotland and meet fluffy cows on the cliffs,
Then cuddle up on a picnic rug as puffins search for fish.

I want to go to Norway and float through fjords so slow,
And visit all the little huts so red against the snow.

I want to go to Iceland and build black sandcastles on the beach,
Then we'll slide along ancient glaciers and see waterfalls too high to reach.

I want to go to Finland because I heard that reindeer live there.
We'll spend our nights gazing at lights in the sky and catch snowflakes in our hair.

I want to go to Germany where fairytales leap off the pages,
Where houses are like gingerbread, and the lakes go on for ages.

I want to go to Switzerland where the mountains stand tall and high,
And roll down grassy slopes with Dad while hearing cowbells passing by.

I want to go to France to sit atop the Eiffel Tower.
Have a picnic with freshly baked macarons and watch as it sparkles on the hour.

I want to go to Spain and dance with people in the street,
Then see buildings of all shapes and colours before we have to escape the heat!

I want to go to Italy and learn how the locals cook.
We'll play hide-and-seek at the Colosseum, a place I've only seen in books.

I want to go to Greece and float in the warm sea of blue,
Get lost exploring the narrow streets and befriend a cat or two!

I have a long, long list of places that I want to see.
And the best part of those places is my family with me.

HUNTER'S SCAVENGER HUNT

There are a lot of things to discover on Hunter's dream holiday to Europe. See if you can find them all!

a waterfall

a plate of scones

a puffin

a cat

the Eiffel Tower

a red hut

a pizza

a cowbell

a reindeer

a dancer

a castle